CW00854633

The Alaska Adventures of Robby and Peter

L. F. Tutt

CROSSBOOKS
PUBLISHING

CrossBooks™
A Division of LifeWay
1663 Liberty Drive
Bloomington, IN 47403
www.crossbooks.com
Phone: 1-866-879-0502

First published by CrossBooks: 11/22/2011

ISBN: 978-1-4627-1108-6 (sc)
ISBN: 978-1-4627-1107-9 (e)

Library of Congress Control Number: 2011917833

Printed in the United States of America

This book is printed on acid-free paper.

Any people depicted in stock imagery provided by Thinkstock are models,
and such images are being used for illustrative purposes only.

Certain stock imagery © Thinkstock.

This book is dedicated to all children who are looking for adventure.

You know who you are and I hope you find it.

Acknowledgements

The author wishes to acknowledge Uproar Graphics, LLC---Chandler Axemaker, uproaralaska@gmail.com for his help with graphic photo enhancement on the cover picture, the cabin picture used for "The Secret of the Old Cabin", and the snowy mountain picture used for "Lost In The Snow".

Contents

The Secret of the Old Cabin

L. F. Tutt

Chapter 1

Looking For Adventure

Haunting loon calls echoed across Mirror Lake, which awakened Robby from a very good night's sleep. He yawned and stretched his arms as far as he could above his head. It was still early, so instead of jumping out of bed, he rolled onto his side to look out the window at God's beautiful creation.

He could see a mallard hen and her ducklings as they swam and splashed near the lakeshore in the soft morning light. Out of the corner of his eye, he caught the flash of a kingfisher bird as it dove into the water after a minnow. He loved to come to his family's rustic lakeside cabin, and this time it was even better, because his best friend Peter was with him.

Thinking of his friend, he looked up at the underside of the bunk above him; the bedsprings stretched and sagged under Peter's weight. Feeling mischievous, Robby pulled his legs out from beneath the blankets, lined his feet up under the lump overhead, and with a laugh gave a powerful push with his legs. Peter yelped as he almost rolled out onto the floor. Every blond hair on Peter's tousled head stuck out as he leaned over the edge of the bunk.

"Hey, what's the big idea?" he asked, as he wiped the sleep from his bright blue eyes.

Robby smiled up at his friend and said, "The big idea is to wake you up, so we can do something fun before the whole day is gone."

"Oh, yeah? Well, one whiff of your breath is enough to wake anybody up!" announced Peter as he jumped down onto the floor.

"My breath!" exclaimed Robby. "My breath is nothing compared to your smelly blasts during the night!"

Laughing, Peter grabbed hold of Robby's blankets and jerked them hard enough to pull Robby half off the bottom bunk. Robby twisted to the right, reached over, took hold of Peter's ankle, and toppled him onto the floor. The boys laughed and wrestled around until Robby's mom called from the kitchen, "I've got some pancakes ready if you boys are hungry."

Quickly untangling themselves, they hopped around while they put on the stained and wrinkled clothes they'd worn the day before. Then, with pushes and shoves they raced each other to the table.

Robby's dad had already eaten most of his pancakes and downed his morning cup of coffee. He looked up as the boys rushed in. "It looks like you two are in a hurry. What do you have planned for today?"

"We'd like to go exploring," Robby said, as he plunked himself down at the table. "Would it be all right if we took the canoe over to Shadow Cove and went on a hike from there?"

"I think that sounds okay," said Dad, with a glance over at Mom for agreement.

"It's fine with me," Mom said. "I'll pack you boys some lunch, since you'll probably get hungry while you're gone."

After a brief, but thankful prayer for the food, the boys dug hungrily into their stacks of pancakes, which they gobbled up with lip-smacking happiness. While they ate, Robby's dad reminded them that they would need some extra gear for their hike through the nearby woods.

The boys finished breakfast, and went out to the shed behind the cabin, where they packed an emergency kit to take along. Their eyes glittered with excitement as Robby grabbed a hatchet with which to mark their trail. Then, into the backpack they added some bug dope, bandages, a length of rope, two pairs of binoculars, and some matches in a waterproof container. Robby's dad came out and inserted three bottles of water and a nice lunch for both boys, plus a couple of protein bars for an emergency snack. They discussed what time the boys needed to be back and checked to see that they had at least one watch between them.

Finally, the boys were ready to go. They trooped down to the dock, and Robby put the pack into the middle of their canoe, while Peter added a couple of fly fishing poles and tackle boxes he'd taken from beside the shed. The boys climbed carefully into the boat, seized their paddles, and swiftly glided away.

After they had rounded the first peninsula, and were out of sight of the cabin, they poked along the shoreline, trying to decide whether to fish on their way over to the cove or on their way back. However, almost at once, their minds were made up for them when Peter saw a big trout surface after a bug.

"Did you see that?" he whispered.

"See what? I didn't see anything."

Pointing toward an abandoned beaver house, Peter said, "Look over there! I just saw a huge trout!"

Robby cupped his hand over his hazel eyes to shield them from the sun, but he could only see the ripples where the trout had been.

The canoe drifted as both boys quietly got their fishing poles ready, and soon they cast their lines over the crystal water of the lake. Above them sunlight sifted through the leaves of the trees, which warmed their backs, while a light breeze ruffled their hair. It was exactly enough wind to keep the mosquitoes away, but not so much that it interfered with casting their flies.

In the underwater shadows, the boys could see some little minnows flash and dart among the rocks and beaver-chewed branches. Some of the minnows began to chase after their colorful flies.

All of a sudden, Robby's pole bent down. This was no minnow on the end of his line! He set the hook, and let out a whoop that echoed around the lake. Intently he fought the fish, reeling in a little of his line at a time. The trout's beautiful red, green, and gold colors flashed as it flipped itself into the air.

Just then, Peter's line sang out as it whizzed from his reel. His fish put up quite a fight, too, first with a deep dive and then high leaps and acrobatic twists, all in an attempt to shake the hook from his mouth.

Robby and Peter landed their fish almost at the same time, and held them up side by side to admire them.

"Hey, let's release these and try for some more tomorrow," said Peter.

"Okay," agreed Robby.

With great care they removed the hooks from their fish's mouths, and then held the trout in the water until they revived. With a flick of their tails, the fish disappeared into the cool depths of the lake.

"Hey, Robby, how about we change places so I can have a chance to steer the canoe?" Peter asked when his fish had swum out of sight.

"Yeah sure, but we'll need to go ashore to make the switch, since I don't want you to dump me in the lake!"

They paddled to a place where they could beach the canoe, and exchanged seats, which put Robby in the front, and Peter in the back steering position. Once they were settled, Robby pushed them from the shore, and right away started to howl with laughter over Peter's uneven attempts to paddle the canoe. With each stroke, Peter pushed the canoe first one way and then the other in a wide zigzag pattern.

"Peter!" Robby exclaimed, doubled over with glee. "At this rate it will be time to go back before we even get there!"

"Don't laugh!" shouted Peter. To make him quit he smacked his paddle onto the surface of the lake, and splashed cold water up Robby's back, and into his dark brown hair. Robby was startled, but thinking fast, he grabbed the can they used for bailing from the bottom of the canoe, scooped up water, and threw it back in Peter's amused face.

"War!" yelled Peter when he could breathe again, and a water fight was on! It lasted until they were both soaked, and there was a good inch of water in the bottom of the rocking canoe.

"I give!" shouted Robby, wiping the water from his eyes.

"Okay," said Peter with a grin, unable to resist just one more, tiny splash with his paddle.

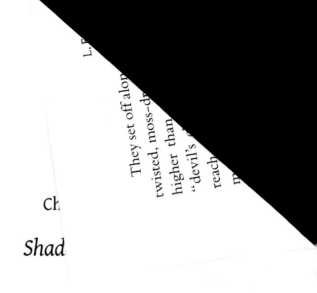

Ch

Shad

After Robby coached Peter on how to paddle the canoe, it wasn't long before they entered Shadow Cove. Though the sun was high in the sky, entering the cove was like going into a dark and gloomy cave. Tall, overgrown trees and thick tangles of brush covered the high hills that enclosed the cove on three sides. The enormous, dense vegetation blocked out most of the light, making the place so unappealing that hardly anyone ever went there. Of course, that was part of the reason why Robby and Peter had picked it as the place to begin their adventure.

The boys stepped ashore, and after they had flipped the canoe to dump the water out, they secured it to a nearby tree with a length of rope. Robby then hid their fishing gear in the bushes, while Peter grabbed the heavy backpack, slung it over his shoulders, and said, "Let's go!"

g a winding path that passed under aped trees and giant ferns that loomed their heads. Beside the trail grew huge lub" plants, which seemed to be trying to out and grab them. The boys detoured around the enacing devil's club to avoid the long, thorny needles which poked out from the stems and undersides of the leaves.

"Wow, this place feels kind of eerie," said Peter.

"Yeah," agreed Robby, looking warily over his shoulder.

To escape the creepy feel of Shadow Cove, they raced up the steep hill. Both boys were out of breath by the time they reached the top, and stopped to look around for a place to rest. Almost right away Robby spotted a sun-bathed log. He plopped down on it and motioned Peter over to sit beside him.

"Man, that was some climb!" said Peter, wiping his face with his T-shirt.

"Yeah," replied Robby, as he rummaged around in the backpack Peter had set on the ground. He hoped to find one of the water bottles he knew were there. When he found one, he took a couple of big gulps, and let some of the cool fresh water dribble down his chin. Then he passed the bottle to Peter, who emptied the rest of it in one long drink.

For a few minutes they sat in silence and just looked around, until all of a sudden, Robby felt the stinging bite of a mosquito. He swiftly swatted it, and smashed its blood-filled body against his arm. At the same time,

Peter slapped the side of his face, as one of the fierce insects began to suck his blood.

"Little vampires!" Peter growled as he snatched the mosquito repellent from their pack. He sprayed himself and then Robby from head to toe, however, more mosquitoes attacked anyway. The little black pests buzzed and swarmed around them, until they couldn't stand it anymore.

"Come on, let's get out of here before they eat us alive!" cried Peter. He stowed the bug dope, and the water bottle, and then grabbed the hatchet out of the outside loop of the pack.

"You're not going to try to kill all these bugs with a hatchet, are you?" joked Robby.

"No, you dufus, I'm going to start to blaze our trail from here!"

With care Peter swung the hatchet, and made a small slash mark on a birch tree near where they had sat. Then he stopped to make another mark about every hundred feet or so, as they bolted down the snake-like path ahead.

For quite a while Peter and Robby hiked wherever the trail took them—around lakes, across small streams, and through dank swamps, always on the lookout for adventure.

As they went, they made note of everything they saw: a bull moose who fed on underwater plants at the edge of a pond, an otter's slide down a steep hill, and a large nest built high in a cottonwood tree. The nest belonged to a pair of eagles, which circled overhead. Right beside the path, they were startled to see where a small bear had recently made scratch marks down the side of a spruce tree. The sap was still fresh from where the bear had sharpened his claws.

The next hill they crested, gave them a great view of a large lake spread out below them. Its surface shimmered and danced in the sunlight, and the reflection was so bright that the boys had to shield their eyes.

"Let's stop here. I could use a rest, and besides, my stomach is shouting that it is time to eat!" Robby said.

"Yeah, mine too!"

The weary boys dropped down on some large, flat rocks, and pulled their lunches out of the backpack. After asking Jesus to bless their food, they devoured the sandwiches, apples, and cookies Robby's mother had packed.

Suddenly, Peter let out a big belch! Laughing, he said, "Yum, it tastes just as good the second time!"

"Gross," Robby mumbled around his last bite of lunch. He pretended to disapprove, but was secretly glad that when they were in the woods they didn't have to mind their manners.

The sun was warm and their bellies were full, so the boys found a place to lie back on the cushy, plant-covered ground. For a while all they did was look up at the puffy clouds, which floated overhead. It was quiet except for the chirping of birds, and the slight rustling sound the leaves made in the breeze.

Peace … Robby thought. He remembered the verse his pastor had read at church last Sunday: Jesus said, "My peace I give you, not as the world gives, I give it to you." Well, this place is peaceful, so it must be a gift from God, he reasoned, feeling right with the Lord and the world.

"Hey," Peter said, "you ready to go?"

"Not yet. I want to scan the area around the lake with my binoculars to see if there is anything interesting or if we should take another trail."

"Okay," said Peter. He got out his binoculars, and handed the other pair to Robby.

Both boys glassed the lake in hopes that they would find something out of the ordinary. At first they didn't see anything; however during his second scan, Robby pointed and exclaimed, "Look over there!" Peter looked, but couldn't see anything to get excited about. Robby gestured toward the other side of the lake, until Peter saw what had made him hyper. It was an old, gray, log cabin almost hidden by brush and other foliage.

"Are you talking about that dingy old cabin?"

"Yeah, let's go explore it; there might be some cool stuff to look at in there!"

The boys packed up their things, and began their hike around to the other side of the lake. The trail followed the shoreline, so it didn't take long to get to the area where they thought the cabin might be. However, everything was so overgrown that it took a while before they found it again. They had to peer through a confusion of devil's club, plus tangled brush and trees, which stood like rows of soldiers between them, and their goal.

Chapter 3

The Old Cabin

Peter looked at Robby and asked, "Wow, how are we going to get in there?"

Robby thought for a minute before he answered, "It looks to me like the only way is to hack a path in with our hatchet."

"I don't know about you, but that doesn't sound like too much fun. Besides, we need gloves so our hands won't get cut to ribbons, and filled with thorns by the time we're done."

Robby glanced at his watch and said, "Well, maybe the thing to do is come back tomorrow with some gloves. Besides, it is awfully close to the time we need to start back, and if we're late my parents won't let us come back here at all."

Their decision made, the boys marched back around the lake, and started to follow the trail they had blazed. Once they reached Shadow Cove, they put their pack and the fishing gear in the canoe. They paddled hard to get across Mirror Lake in record time, because they couldn't wait to tell about what they had found.

However, when they were halfway to shore, Robby stopped paddling and said, "Hey Peter, hold up, I want to talk. I've been thinking that we may not want to tell my folks about the cabin. I mean, I don't like to keep things from my parents, but I think it would be more fun to explore the old cabin without my dad. If we tell him, I'm sure he'll want to go back with us."

"Yeah, it would be more fun if it was just the two of us."

"Let's just tell them about all the other things we saw and did today, but not about our big find."

The boys agreed, and once again began to paddle toward the cabin.

Robby's mom and dad came out to greet them as they tied up to the dock.

"Did you boys have a good time?"

"You bet," the boys replied with big grins.

They unloaded the boat and went up the dock with their gear. They couldn't wait to share their adventures. In their excitement they talked over each other, as they told about the fish they had caught, and all the lakes, ponds, streams, and critters they had seen. Peter almost let it slip about the log cabin they'd found, but he caught himself just in time. Robby changed the subject, and thanked his mom for the good lunch she'd made for them.

"Yeah," Peter chimed in. "It was really great!"

The rest of the day was spent doing a few chores, and then they played their favorite games. While Robby was beating Peter at Monopoly, his mother brought them delicious, lake-chilled root beer floats, and a bowl full of popcorn to enjoy.

Just before bedtime Robby said, "Dad, we'd like to explore again tomorrow."

"Are you sure that's what you'll want to do? It looks like the weather is going to be nice and sunny again. Wouldn't you'd rather go swimming instead or do a little more fishing?"

"No, we'd really rather explore; we can fish and swim any old time."

Robby's mom and dad exchanged smiles, then his dad said, "It's okay if you go, particularly since you were careful today, and you even got back ahead of time. We'll send another lunch along with you. Is there anything else you'll need?"

The boys looked at each other, and then Robby asked, "Could we have a couple pairs of gloves? We ran into some devil's club, and you know what that's like."

While Robby's dad went to the shed to bring them each a pair of heavy-duty work gloves, Robby couldn't help feeling a little ashamed. He liked being totally honest with his dad and, yeah, it wasn't technically lying, but he hadn't told him the whole story either. He silenced his conscience with the thought that he and Peter weren't planning to do anything wrong.

Later that night when the boys went to bed, they whispered about the adventure they'd had, and about their plans for tomorrow. Both of them were sure they were too excited to sleep; however, before they knew it, they were dead to the world.

The next morning was perfect for their adventure. They gobbled down their breakfast, grabbed the stuff they needed, and soon had the nose of the canoe pointed toward Shadow Cove.

Today they didn't stop to fish, and before long they were there. They pulled the canoe up onto the beach, and shouldered their gear in anticipation of the adventure ahead. They didn't linger on the trail, and once they had crested the top of the first hill, they hurried along watching for the blaze marks Peter had made the day before. It seemed like no time at all until they were in front of the stand of devil's club that stood between them and the old cabin.

Robby sat down on a nearby stump to catch his breath, and take a long drink from his water bottle. Peter took a drink, too, and then reached into the backpack to get the gloves and hatchet.

"We should have brought another hatchet," said Peter ruefully.

"Yeah, I thought about it, but my dad might have been suspicious if we asked for another one. I figured that whenever we get tired, we can just trade off."

"Hey, can I go first?" cried Peter.

"Sure, but before you begin swinging away, let's find the shortest path."

The boys climbed up on a large rock that was nearby, trying to see the entrance to the cabin.

"I think I can kind of make out where it is," Robby said.

"Where the devil's club is a little shorter than the rest of the bushes?" asked Peter.

"Yeah, I think that looks like the way to go."

The boys hopped down and put on gloves, and Peter began to chop. As Peter chopped, Robby pulled the devil's club out of the way, and stacked it to the side. It was tough work, because there were some pretty big alder, and willow bushes mixed in, and all the foliage was springy, and hard to cut with the hatchet.

It wasn't long before Peter was worn out, and handed off the hatchet to Robby with a tired grin. They worked for about an hour, and made good progress, but they were exhausted and thirsty, so they decided to take a break.

"Hey, let's go eat part of our lunch down on that log by the lake. We can sit there, and cool our feet in the water."

The boys didn't talk much for a few minutes, while they munched on their sandwiches. Once they had more energy, they compared scratch marks they'd gotten on their arms, and discussed how much longer it would take to reach the cabin.

"What do you think we'll find in the cabin?" Peter asked.

"I don't know, I suppose it will depend on whether anyone else has been in it lately. I've heard that sometimes people find cool stuff like knives, clothes, and even old coins, but sometimes the cabins are just empty, too."

"It would be awesome to find a knife, or maybe even an old hatchet," said Peter. "What would you like to find?"

"Oh, I don't know, maybe some old maps or books."

After they'd finished their lunch, it was easy to get started again, especially now that they were able to see the cabin through the jumble of brush that still blocked their way. Another hour of hard work and the boys were standing at the log cabin's only door. It was weathered, and had very rusty hinges. The handle, they noticed, was formed from part of an old moose antler, which Peter grabbed and gave a sharp tug. However, the door didn't open.

"Here, let me help you," said Robby, grasping the handle, too. On the count of three, they pulled together, but they still couldn't budge the door.

"Hey, what's the deal, why won't it open?" asked Peter.

"I don't know," answered Robby, taking off one of his gloves, and scratching his head. Together they began checking out the door, and it didn't take long to realize that the hinges were rusted solid.

"What are we going to do now?" asked Peter.

"Beats me," answered Robby in a frustrated voice, "but after that much hard work a couple of rusty hinges aren't going to keep me out!"

The boys threaded their way around the cabin, in search of another means to get inside. It looked like their only option was to pry open one of the shuttered windows near the door.

"I think we may be able to get in if we can figure out how to get the shutters off this window," said Robby.

"I know, let's use the hatchet," said Peter. "It's the only thing that might be tough enough to pry them open."

After a lot of grunts and groans made by the boys, as they struggled to remove one of the shutters, it finally splintered at its hinges and fell to the ground. In another moment, Robby and Peter were peering through dirty glass into the dim interior of the cabin.

The shadows cast by all the trees and brush around the outside made it hard to see much of anything at first. However, once their eyes adjusted to the murky light, they could make out the room on the other side of the grimy window. It was a smallish space that contained a living, dining, and kitchen area all in one room.

"You know," said Robby, "I can see some great stuff in there."

"Yeah," replied Peter, "let's move this sliding window and go inside." Grabbing hold of the edge of the window, both boys shoved with all their might, in expectation that it would stick like the door. Instead, the window almost broke, because it wasn't latched, and flew open. Peter went in first, with Robby breathing down his neck, eager to explore the mysterious cabin.

Chapter 4

The Secret

Right away, they could see that no one had been there for a long time. As they explored they noticed the strong smells of dust, and mold, and mildew, which meant water had leaked in somewhere.

"Pee-ewe! It sure stinks in here," said Peter, wrinkling his nose.

"Yeah," Robby replied, as he batted at some cobwebs that dangled in his face, "but it's still awesome!"

Robby looked around some more, and then reached over and picked up a dusty can from the countertop. "Hey, look at this label. They don't make this brand anymore," he said as he held it out for Peter's inspection. The outside of the can had an old, faded label showing a pot of pork and beans.

"I love pork and beans, but I don't think I'd want to eat what's in this can, it might make me explode.

"You mean more than usual?" asked Peter with a grin.

The boys didn't talk for a while as they checked out all the drawers, shelves, and bins, and absorbed the old-time feel of the cabin and its contents.

"Did you see all the mouse droppings everywhere?" asked Peter, pointing to a pile and a nest he'd seen in a nearby corner.

"Yuck, they're probably part of the reason it reeks in here."

In the kitchen cupboards they'd found more canned goods, as well as some plates, bowls, and drinking glasses. Under the counter there were some hard-to-open, metal-topped containers, which held stale flour, sugar, cereal, and rice.

In the drawers they found silverware, a can opener, candles, and some other odds and ends.

"Wow, look at this old knife," said Peter, lifting it from another drawer. "This is just what I'd hoped I'd find!"

"Cool," said Robby.

Together they studied an intricate carving of a moose on its bone handle, and admired the curve of its partially rusted blade. They set the knife on the table, thinking that maybe later they would take it home with them as a souvenir.

Next they looked in wooden boxes, which had been stacked to form shelves near a mouse-infested easy chair. The boxes contained a lot of old magazines. Some of the magazines had been chewed, and soiled by the mice, but others were okay.

"Hey, look at the date on this *Alaska Magazine*—it says June of 1988."

"Wow that was really a long time ago! Do you think it could have been the last time anyone was here?"

"I don't know it's kind of hard to tell."

"Yeah," said Peter pointing to his left. "Let's search the rest of the cabin. I want to see what is over behind that door."

Together the boys walked over to what appeared to be the only other room. Peter took hold of the doorknob, and cautiously turned it. He gave the door a push, and it slowly swung open, making an eerie, creaking sound.

"It's sort of dark in there; I can't see much," he said, peering into the room. Little bits of light filtered down through a caved-in portion of the ceiling. The boys hesitated for a moment while their eyes adjusted to the dimness, then they stepped farther and farther into the gloom.

In the shadowy light they saw the shapes of broken rafters, which must have buckled under a heavy snow load in some long-ago winter. The boys noticed that when the roof caved in, part of it had fallen on a small desk and chair. Over to their right, they could see a closet. Peter went over to it, and slowly opened the door to discover what was inside. His heart skipped a couple of beats when he thought he saw someone standing in the darkness, but it turned out to be just an old hat and a moth-eaten wool jacket hanging there.

Besides the hat, and the jacket, there were some ratty looking sheets, and a chewed-up spare blanket on one of the shelves. Lying in a heap on the floor were some more old clothes, but because of the mice neither boy wanted to poke around in them.

After he finished exploring the closet, Peter said, "I'd sure like to take a peek to see what's in the desk over there." It was the one that the roof had collapsed on, and the top had been crushed into the only drawer. "Here, help me shift this junk."

The two boys pushed with all their might, but they couldn't budge the heavy broken beams.

"It looks like we won't be able to move these on our own," said Robby, panting from exertion.

"Maybe we can just pry the drawer front off with the hatchet."

"Yeah, that's a good idea. Wait here while I go get it," said Robby. "I think we left it outside on the ground below the window."

Peter waited in the strange, spooky light, feeling a chill walk up his back with icy fingers. He hadn't wanted to tell Robby that ever since they'd come into the bedroom, he'd felt a little scared. What he didn't know was that Robby was feeling the same way, and was glad to get out of there for a few minutes. Before long, though, Robby returned with the hatchet, and they began prying on the drawer. When they got the front off, they still couldn't see anything in the murky light.

"I'm not sure I want to put my hand in there after all the mice mess we've seen."

"I'll reach in there with my gloves on," volunteered Peter, pulling them out of his back pocket to feel around in the dark recesses of the drawer. The first thing he brought out was an old leather belt. The leather was kind of moldy, but it had a cool, gold-colored buckle with some kind of fish engraved on it. Next, he pulled out a few dried-up pens, which he dropped without interest onto the floor. He felt around some more, but only succeeded in stirring up a bunch of dust.

"It looks like that's all there is," said Peter with a sneeze.

"Okay, but while we're here, let's have a last look around. I'm not sure I want to come back in here once we go out."

"I know what you mean; it feels kind of creepy!"

While he was talking, Peter stepped back and bumped into the single bed that was set under a shuttered window. He caught his balance by steadying himself against the wall, which put him in position to view the empty bed more clearly—but it wasn't empty like he had expected. Instead, what he saw wrapped his chest in bands of fear! Robby looked toward the bed at the same time; and when he did, every hair on his head seemed to stand straight up. It felt like a bucket of icy water had been dumped over him! The boys gasped, dropped everything on the floor, and raced out of the bedroom. They dashed through the main room over to the window and leaped out, almost landing on top of each other, in their hurry.

Chapter 5

Secret Solved

Peter and Robby sprinted as fast as they could down the path to the lake. Robby's teeth were chattering, and Peter was running his fingers through his hair over and over.

"D-did you s-see what I s-saw?" stuttered Robby.

Peter nodded his head yes, and then whispered, "I think I saw a skeleton on the bed!"

Robby shuddered, glancing back at the cabin, half expecting to see something ghostly float through the window. His mind told him that his fears were silly, but his pounding heart said otherwise.

"W-what are we going to do?" Peter asked. "I don't know if I want to go back in there, not even to get the hatchet that we dropped when we ran out!" Suddenly, his legs gave way, and he abruptly sat down on a log behind him.

The boys thought for a minute about what they should do. Finally, Robby said, "I think we are going to be in a lot of trouble for going in that old cabin."

Peter replied defensively, "I didn't see any 'No Trespassing' signs anywhere. And besides, we didn't damage anything."

"Yeah, right!" said Robby sarcastically. "We only ripped a shutter off the window of a closed-up cabin. You're not supposed to do that unless you're stranded, starving, or lost. Remember, it's one of the rules my dad taught us about exploring in the Alaska wilds. Plus, we tore the front off that old desk, and that's destroying property, too!"

Peter began to look kind of guilty, and Robby was already feeling that way. No matter how they examined their actions, they knew that what they had done was wrong. It was one thing to go in an abandoned cabin where everything was almost completely tumbled down, and the door was hanging off its hinges; but to go in where a place was locked up tight—that was trespassing.

Peter said, "I don't suppose you would want to just race in the bedroom, get the hatchet, and then put the shutter back like we had never been here?"

"Yeah, that is what I'd like to do, but then what are we going to tell my parents we did all day?"

"I don't know, but just this once couldn't we kind of not lie, but not tell the whole story?" asked Peter.

"No, I don't think that would be right, besides you and I always look guilty when we've done something wrong. Plus, we can't just overlook the fact that there's a skeleton in there.

"I guess you're probably right, but I'm not going to enjoy telling this to your folks."

Robby got up, walked slowly back to the cabin, closed the window, and leaned the broken shutter against the outside wall. Then he returned to where Peter was sitting, picked up the pack, and said miserably, "I think we might as well go back now, and face my mom and dad."

Peter paused for a moment to take a long look at the old cabin, and wished to himself they'd never found it.

The trip back was a blur. Even though they drug their feet all the way, it seemed like only moments before they were home. The boys took their time docking the canoe, and gathering up their gear to take it inside. They even tried to put off seeing Robby's parents, by going directly to the bunkroom via the back door.

However, Robby's dad heard them come in, and walked into the room to ask how their day had been. The boys looked so guilty that he knew immediately something was wrong.

He instantly asked, "What's the matter?"

Neither boy answered, so Robby's dad said, "Okay boys, let's go into the kitchen, and talk about what's been going on."

Robby's mom was in the process of making supper when she saw the cheerless procession come in. She turned down the heat under the stew, dried her hands on a dish towel, and sat down with her husband across the dining table from the boys.

Robby was so upset that Peter decided to be brave, and help out his friend by telling what had happened. However, as soon as he got started with the story, Robby began to add details he thought Peter was missing. In the meantime, Robby's parents began to be extremely unhappy the more of their tale the boys told. However, that was nothing compared to their startled faces, when they heard about the skeleton.

Robby finished the story and added, "We're really sorry. We didn't mean to do something so wrong. I guess we just got carried away in our excitement."

Robby's parents sat still, and looked back and forth at each other, while they thought of what to say to the boys. Finally, Robby's dad said, "Well, I need to look into this matter with you, but there isn't enough time left today. We'll leave for the old cabin right after breakfast tomorrow, and then we'll discuss this, and figure out what to do from there."

The boys nodded their agreement, while they exchanged anxious glances at each other. There was no way they wanted to go back to the cabin again! And they knew no matter what happened they were in a lot of trouble.

For the boys, the rest of the evening dragged by, with everyone heading to bed early. Peter and Robby lay on their bunks, and thought about what they had found that day. They went over and over in their minds the moment when they had spotted the skeleton in the dim corner. Neither boy wanted to talk about how afraid they'd been. It wasn't until after the "midnight sun" had finally set around one o'clock in the morning that they drifted into a restless, uneasy sleep.

The next morning they left as planned, but not with any of the excitement that they'd felt before. Robby's dad was not talking, and the boys knew by the set of his jaw that he was still upset.

Before long they reached the cabin. The boys hung back while Robby's dad walked around surveying what they had done.

"I'm going to go in now and look around, he said. Tell me, where was the skeleton you found?"

Robby pointed to the east end of the cabin as his dad took out the flashlight he had brought, moved the propped-up shutter, opened the window, and slipped inside. The boys watched him as he walked around the main room, before he moved out of sight into the bedroom. Neither boy realized that they were holding their breath while they listened to the eerie creaking of the floorboards under his feet. Brief flickers from his flashlight shone through chinks in the logs, especially from the corner where the skeleton lay.

It seemed like forever, but it really wasn't long before Robby's dad came to the window with a strange look on his face. He said, "I want you boys to come in here." Robby and Peter looked at each other in dismay; the last thing they wanted to do was go back inside. "Come on boys," Robby's dad said more firmly. So, Robby first, and then Peter reluctantly swung their legs over the windowsill, and climbed into the main room.

The hair was beginning to stand up on Peter's neck as he said, "Please sir, I don't want to go back into that room."

Robby's dad responded, "I hope you will trust me when I say that you really have to go back in there in order to solve this mystery once and for all." So with feet dragging, they followed him into the darkness.

The boys stood in back of him, shuddering as they looked toward the corner where the skeleton lay. Then Robby's dad shone his flashlight on the bed— and instead of a skeleton, what they saw made them burst out laughing in relief. On the bed was a bunch of branches, moth-eaten clothing, and an old broken lantern. The lantern had a frosted globe, which they had mistaken for a skull in the dim light the day before. Some branches had landed on the bed, when the roof caved in years ago, and the way everything had fallen, mixed with the clothing, and blankets, had made the boys believe a skeleton lay there in the dusky light.

Robby's dad retrieved the hatchet and belt from the floor, while the boys turned and headed for the living area. They sat on the edge of a couple of chairs at the dining table grinning at one another, really happy that there hadn't been a skeleton in there after all. Robby's dad, however, was not as happy.

"Boys," he said standing by the table, "I am really glad that things have worked out this way, but there is still the matter of the damage you did when you forced your way in here. I'm not exactly sure how you are going to repair the damage you've done, but you will complete it before the summer is over. Also, I expect you to put everything back as close as you can to the way it was."

"Yes sir," Robby and Peter said in unison.

Robby got up, and went back into the bedroom to return the belt to the desk drawer along with the pens scattered on the floor, while Peter put back the bone-handle knife. In the meantime, Robby's dad looked over what had been broken, and made a mental list of supplies they would need to bring with them for repairs the next time they came to their cabin on Mirror Lake.

As they left, they secured everything as much as they could, even piling brush back onto the path so that the log cabin would be less noticeable.

When they got home, the boys had to endure the lecture of their young lives. Their heads were hanging, by the time the scolding was over.

"Mom, Dad, I am so sorry for not obeying you. I promise not to do anything so stupid again," said Robby.

"Me too," said Peter, with a sad hang-dog look on his face.

"We forgive you," said Robby's parents, as they gave each of the boys a hug.

Right then, the boys also took time to pray, and ask Jesus to forgive them. After their prayers were finished, both Peter and Robby felt so much better. They knew though that they wouldn't truly have the whole thing behind them, until they had put everything back the way it had been at the old cabin.

After a time, the boys wandered out to sit on the dock. Peter began tossing leaves onto the lake. He'd pulled them off a tree branch on his way from the cabin. He sat and watched them swirl away on the breeze, which tickled the surface of the lake.

Robby sat and drug his feet back and forth through the water, looking sad. He was thinking, how not only had his parents been disappointed, but the Lord must have been disappointed, too. God wasn't harsh or mean, but He did want His children to be thoughtful and caring about others. Breaking into a cabin, even if it was old and appeared to be abandoned, was not the right thing to do. Deep down in his heart, he'd known it the whole time.

Peter looked over at his friend, and realized from the look on his face, that their thoughts were probably about the same things. However, never one to dwell on stuff for long he came up with a plan to cheer up his friend. Taking the remainder of the leaves he still had in his hand he dumped them onto Robby's head. Robby batted them all off, except for a few, which he tried to shove down the back of Peter's shirt. Peter twisted to get away, and the next thing he knew he had fallen in the cool water of the lake. He came up and gasped for air. Then, not hesitating for a moment, he pulled Robby in with him.

After the splashing died down, Robby and Peter heard laughter from over by the cabin. They looked and saw that it was Robby's dad and mom enjoying the silly antics of the boys.

"Hey dad, will you come over to the dock and help us get out? My jeans feel like they weigh a ton."

"Sure," his dad said. He walked over, and reached down to help Robby up, but instead Robby grabbed his arm for more leverage, and pulled him in, too. Now everyone laughed, especially Robby's mom, who said, "Don't even think about trying that on me."

"Ah, come on in, the water's not cold," coaxed her husband.

"I know better than that!" she exclaimed. She turned, and headed for the cabin to get a bar of soap, some clean towels, and dry clothes for each of them.

"Here," she said a few moments later, while she put the supplies down on the dock. "You might as well get clean while you're at it. I'm going to finish supper, so just come on up when you're done."

There weren't any other people at the lake that weekend, so the guys stripped down and took a bath right then and there. By the time they got out, they were clean, but so cold their lips were blue and their teeth were chattering. They hurriedly dried off, dressed, and then ran into the cabin to sit by the warm woodstove.

That evening Robby's mom let the boys eat their supper picnic style on the floor, so they could stay where it was warm. While they ate, they studied some of the maps of the area, and planned a fishing adventure for the next day. They couldn't decide whether to fish their lake or go to another one, where few people ever fished. The boys playfully squabbled back and forth about what they should do, until it was time for bed.

As they settled down in their bunks for the night, they talked for a while about what had happened, but they were pretty tuckered out from the events of the past two days.

Robby's last thoughts, as he drifted off to sleep, weren't about the fish he might catch tomorrow, but about the adventure he'd had with his friend. He doubted anything as exciting as that would ever happen again. However, he thought, next time whatever we do, I want to do things the right way … God's way.

What Robby couldn't foresee was an adventure coming, in the months ahead, that would severely test his father's, his friend's, and his own faith in God, and might ultimately cost him his life.

Lost in the Snow

L. F. Tutt

Chapter 1

Get Your Motors Running

"Christmas vacation has sure been a blast!" exclaimed Peter.

"Yeah," replied Robby, "but I'm bummed that it's almost over, and we have to go back to school in two days."

"Well, at least we have one more adventure—the snow-machine* trip planned for tomorrow with your dad and his friends."

The boys were excited about the expedition, so all they did until bedtime was thumb through snowmobile magazines, and study maps of the area they would explore the next day.

The following morning, the stillness was shattered by the harsh, blare of Robby's alarm clock, which jarred the boys awake.

---

* Most Alaskans refer to their snowmobiles as snow-machines.

"Hey," Peter yelled at his friend. "Would you shut that thing off? I'm trying to sleep."

"Sleep?" exclaimed Robby as he leaped out of bed. "You want to sleep on a great morning like this?"

Peter's head popped out from beneath the covers, and a brilliant smile spread across his face as he remembered the reason why he had spent the night with Robby. Bounding out of bed, he ran to the window with his friend to peer out. They stood with their fingers crossed, in hopes they wouldn't see a blinding blizzard or that there had been a Chinook,* either of which would spoil their snow-machine trip. Happily for them, only a few snowflakes slowly sifted down from a thinly overcast sky.

Peter let out a whoop as he pumped his arm in the air and hollered, "Yes! The weather looks awesome!"

"Yeah, and I can't wait to get out in it," replied Robby, running to put on his outdoor clothes.

The boys looked funny as they hopped around, trying to pull on their skintight, long underwear. Robby pointed at Peter and said, "Your long johns look like girls' tights!"

"Yeah," laughed Peter. "Well, you look like a ballet dancer."

Eventually they quit clowning around, and put their energy into getting on their final layers of clothes—turtleneck sweaters, polar fleece vests, and blue jeans. Sweat was beaded on their foreheads by the time they

---

* A Chinook is a warming, melting trend during winter months, usually accompanied by high wind.

had on all the clothes needed for Alaska's harsh winter weather.

"I'll race you," hollered Peter as he pushed his friend out of the way, and ran recklessly down the hall. They skidded to a halt at the breakfast table, where they saw that Robby's mom already had their places set with steaming piles of scrambled eggs, homemade biscuits, and reindeer sausage. After a heartfelt prayer for their food, and the wonderful day, they gobbled down their breakfast. When they were almost done, Robby asked his mother, "Where's Dad?"

"Your dad and his friends are out in the driveway loading the snow-machines for your trip. He said he wanted you to hurry, because they're almost ready to go."

That was all the boys needed to hear. They jumped up, put their dishes in the sink, and then charged toward the door as they struggled into their insulated snowmobile suits.

"Don't forget the rest of your gear," called Robby's mom.

"Okay, we won't. Bye!" the boys hollered in unison.

They headed toward the door, and grabbed a large duffle bag on their way, which contained helmets, gloves, and face masks they would want later.

Out in the yard the arctic winter air smacked them in the face with its icy cold hand, and quick-froze the inside of their nostrils. The snow sparkled like diamonds in the mellow glow cast by the yard light, while underfoot it crunched loudly as they walked toward the truck.

The boys paused for a moment, and tried to catch a few snowflakes on their tongues, until Robby's dad called out, "Okay boys, we're all waiting!"

They quit goofing off, and piled into the back seat of the pickup. As soon as the boys were buckled in, Robby's dad pulled out of the driveway in pursuit of his friends, who were already barreling down the highway to adventure.

The trip up into the mountains of Miners Pass was about an hour from Robby's home, but to the boys the drive seemed to be taking forever, especially since they were eager to get out into the snow filled landscape.

As they drove through the semidarkness of the winter morning, the lightly falling snow gradually stopped, and the clouds thinned out to expose a few stars. Peter, looked out the side window, and could see a small, frozen stream; its summer song trapped in the ice and snow of winter.

A few minutes later, Robby's dad cried out excitedly, "Hey guys, look to your right, there are a couple of moose!" Robby and Peter could see them, in the light cast by the truck's high beams. The moose munched on a breakfast of frozen willow branches. The boys could see their big jaws grinding away on the chewy wood. When they heard the vehicles, they pricked their enormous ears forward to listen. Then they whirled away and ran until they'd disappeared from sight over a nearby ridge. The boys watched as their long lanky legs and large hooves kicked up globs of snow.

Robby smiled at their antics, and thought about how much he treasured the quiet beauty of Alaska. He loved all the remarkable and varied wild animals, majestic mountains, and vast wilderness areas, where a rather small number of people lived. It was a place you could easily see God's handiwork all around you.

The boys began to wiggle in their seats. They knew they must be close to the takeoff point. Finally, after a few more miles, they heard Robby's dad say the words they'd been waiting for: "We're here!"

They looked ahead, and could see everyone parked in a large plowed area surrounded by huge snow berms. "Come on boys, let's go!" Robby's dad said, as he jumped down from the cab of the truck, with the boys close behind him.

Robby paused for a moment, inhaled deeply, and said, "Mmm, I love the smell of fresh snow."

"Me too," agreed Peter with a big grin, "especially when it's mixed with the smell of snow-machine exhaust."

Robby's dad and his friends began readying the machines, while the boys got on their gear, including the cool racing helmets they'd received for Christmas.

The machines screamed to life one by one, and were then quickly off-loaded from the snowmobile trailers with clangs, bangs, and thumps filling the air. The boys ran over to help in any way they could, and soon were astride their machines. Peter was so excited that he bounced up and down.

Power and noise blasted the silence of the frosty air as they revved their engines in anticipation. Robby's dad came over to shout a few last-minute instructions: "Stick close, and don't venture too far off the trail. There are a lot of hazards around here, more than you know. I don't want anything to happen to you."

"Okay!" the boys yelled together over the rumble of the snow-machines. Robby's dad ran over and jumped on his machine, and with a quick look back at the boys, he shot like a rocket after the rest of their group into the snow-filled Alaskan wilderness.

Chapter 2

Headed for Adventure

Robby and Peter dropped the visors on their helmets, which locked them into a world of their own. Throttling up their motors, they roared off after Robby's dad, the snow rooster-tailing up behind them. Ice crystals hung in the air above the trail as they zoomed up the valley. Straight ahead morning's gentle light began to bathe the mountains in pink and gold.

Most of the men didn't stick to the main path; instead they made big looping patterns along the hillsides. It looked like so much fun that the boys decided to try it, too. Peter gunned his engine, and then turned his machine up an embankment. He had to lean his body weight uphill to keep his snow-machine from rolling over. When he reached the top, he zipped back down the hill, crisscrossed the trail, and hit the rise on the other side. For a few seconds he was airborne. Then he landed with a thump, and stopped to watch Robby.

Robby had just completed his big loop, he gunned his motor to get the most out of the jump that Peter had just taken, but he hit the ridge at an angle. Instead of flying up in the air as he expected, he smashed through a lip of snow, half burying himself in the process. Peter raised his visor, and Robby could see he was laughing.

"Way to go!" Peter shouted, his voice dripping with sarcasm.

Robby grabbed a handful of snow, and threw it right at Peter's face. Peter turned his head just in time, so he only got a little snow inside his helmet. He didn't have time to even the score, though, before Robby side slipped his machine off the embankment, and zipped away. Everyone was having a blast as they jumped and raced their way up into the mountains.

In a little over three hours, they reached a high plateau that led into a sheltered valley. The boys recognized where they were, though they'd never been there before in winter.

Peter gave his machine more gas to catch up with Robby. Along the way he spotted the upper story of a dilapidated, old mine building, which poked up out of the snow. It was the same two-story structure they had explored the previous summer, with Robby's dad. When Peter caught up with Robby, he gestured and pointed toward the old building he'd seen. Together the boys idled closer to inspect the mostly buried structure.

They parked as close as they dared, and found they were able to see through some broken windows. From their vantage point, they saw some old bunk beds, mangled mattresses, and miscellaneous junk strewn around.

Robby said, "This is cool! Remember, we never got to see what was up here, on the top floor of this building, last summer. The stairs were way too rickety."

"Yeah," replied Peter. "I can't get over how deep the snow must be for us to be able to look inside like this."

They talked for a few more minutes. Suddenly, they realized it had been some time since they had heard the other snow-machines. The boys glanced around, and saw some of the group were high-marking*, over on some steep hills, while the others watched.

The boys knew that high marking was risky, because sometimes the snow on a hillside could be unstable, and at any moment an avalanche could crash down the mountain. Occasionally, even good riders misjudged the snow conditions, and were overtaken, and buried in the onrushing snow.

As they watched, the men began to assemble in a group to talk. Robby's dad waved at them to come over and join them. The boys turned their machines, and roared back onto the trail, which lead to the knoll where the men were gathered. Once they were together, they began to race out of the valley shadows toward a brightly lit bench of snow.

---

* High marking with a snow-machine is a thrilling contest. Whoever reaches the highest point on the flank of the mountain, without rolling their snow-machine, wins.

Robby and Peter were the last to shut off their machines, and take off their helmets to enjoy the warmth of the sun and the deep stillness that surrounded them. The only things that could be heard were the click-click of the engines as they cooled in the chilly mountain air, and the soft sighs of a light wind.

One of the men said, "I vote we stop here and eat some lunch before we ride any farther." Everyone agreed, especially Peter and Robby, because by this time it had been over four hours since they'd eaten breakfast.

All the men piled off their machines to get at the food packs, which were stowed in rear compartments. It was no trouble to walk around, because the snow on the ridge was windblown and hard packed. However, down in the valley, the snow was much softer, and if you got off your machine there, you'd probably sink up to your waist.

The boys watched Robby's dad unpack a feast of bottled juice, chips, apples, and cookies. He handed them some hot dog buns and packets of ketchup before he went to the front of his machine, and lifted the hood. The boys looked at each other, wondering what in the world he was about to do. Then they saw that clamped to the machine's muffler were some tins, which he carefully removed, and brought back to the boys. When the tins were opened, they saw six hot dogs cooked to perfection, steaming in the frosty air.

"Wow!" said Peter. "This is great!"

Robby was already stuffing his face, so he could only mumble his agreement around a mammoth mouthful.

After he had munched his food for a few minutes, he paused long enough to say, "I thought nothing could beat those burgers we ate at the lake last summer."

"Yeah, I know what you mean, but I don't think anything has ever hit the spot like this!"

While they looked out at the incredible view the men talked, and laughed, and finished their lunches. Everyone enjoyed the spring like warmth of the sun, and was awed by the tall, jagged mountains stretched along the horizon. The peaks jutted up like razor-sharp teeth, which pierced the navy blue sky.

After a while, one of the men called out to Robby's dad, pointing with some concern at dark clouds, which had begun to form along the skyline to the east. "I think we'd better keep an eye on those; it could mean a storm is coming," he said.

To the boys the clouds didn't really look like much of a threat, but they both knew from experience, that winter storms could build rapidly, and without a great deal of warning. They only hoped that this wouldn't be one of those times, because it would mean a quick end to their adventure. Everyone agreed to keep a close watch—just in case.

Robby's dad turned, looked over at Robby and Peter, and asked, "Are you boys having a good time?"

"I sure am!" Robby said with enthusiasm.

"Me too!" Peter chimed in with a big smile.

"Well, we're going to get underway again soon, so remember to keep me in sight like you did on the way up here."

Everyone began to put things away, and were ready to go again in no time. However, before they got started, Robby's dad paused, and asked everyone to bow their heads in prayer.

"Lord, we want to thank You for a safe and fun trip thus far. Please continue to keep us safe, and we thank You for the food we have just enjoyed. Truly You are great! In Jesus' name we pray, Amen."

With the hearty "Amen" still ringing in the air, everyone started their machines for the next leg of the trip. Little did they know what difficulties lay ahead.

Chapter 3

Lost

With their helmets strapped on, and all the engines gunning loudly, Robby couldn't tell whether his machine was revving or not. It wasn't until everyone else had jumped off the ridge, and raced away like horses out of a starting gate, that he knew his engine wasn't running. He turned the key off and on a couple of times, and it still wouldn't start. He glanced up, and saw everyone had zoomed away, and realized that no one had even looked back to see if he was with them, not even Peter. He tried the key again and again, and still nothing happened. He hit the seat in frustration, and hollered, "Stupid machine!"

Again he looked out, and saw that everyone had already made it halfway across the valley. *What am I going to do?* He thought anxiously, as he turned the key again and again and only got a click for his efforts.

It was then that Robby paused, bowed his helmeted head, closed his eyes, and breathed a silent prayer to the Lord for help. When he opened his eyes, the first thing he noticed was the "kill switch," which was in the off position. He quickly pulled it up, and turned the key. Like music to his ears, he heard the engine roar to life.

"Thank You, Lord!" Robby exclaimed, as he pulled down his visor, and rapidly began to follow the direction that everyone else had taken.

He hurtled along the trail as swiftly as he dared. *Wow, I've never gone this fast before*, he thought, as he watched the speedometer climb upward ... fifty, sixty, seventy ... and still he went faster! The speedometer continued to climb, until he was going eighty miles per hour. It was scary, but fun at the same time.

He leaned his body down below the windshield; like he'd seen the other guys do, to create as little wind resistance as possible. At the faster pace, it wasn't long before he reached the mouth of the valley. He looked ahead as far as he could see, then to the left, and then to the right. However, Robby couldn't see anyone, and realized he had no clue as to where they might have gone.

He tried not to worry as he slowed down to examine the snow-machine tracks that crisscrossed all around him in every direction. In fact, there were so many that it was impossible to figure out for sure which route the group had taken.

Robby paused to consider his options. *The guys probably went higher up into the mountains. If that's true, they can't be very far ahead of me. If I keep going fast, I should catch up with them pretty soon.* Tucking his head below his windshield again, he gave his engine full throttle, and headed at top speed in the direction he imagined they had gone.

While Robby tried to catch up, the clouds they had noticed earlier wrapped around the mountaintops, and the front edge of an enormous storm now loomed overhead. Extra-large flakes of snow began to spit out of the gray, gauzelike clouds. The flakes rapidly accumulated all around, only to be picked up by swirling gusts of wind, and blown away again. The snowstorm began to create a dense veil, which blocked out many of the landmarks that would commonly be used to find the way home. The storm swept into the mountain passes, while its charcoal colored clouds formed thick layers, which diminished the light. Soon, everyone had to turn on their headlights to be able see where they were headed.

The group of snow-machiners stopped and bunched close together. They shut down their engines to talk over what to do, now that the storm had arrived. They needed to discuss whether they had time to ride some more or if they should go back to their trucks.

It was during their conversation that Peter looked around, and concluded he hadn't seen Robby since lunch. He'd assumed that he was in the group somewhere, racing ahead or jumping with his dad, but he certainly wasn't with them now.

Peter interrupted the conversation and asked, "Has anyone seen Robby?" Everyone looked around, even back in the direction they had come, but he was not in the area.

Robby's dad replied anxiously, "I guess I haven't seen my son since we stopped earlier."

All the men started to discuss the problem. "I vote we stick together, and head straight back the way we came," said one of the men.

"Yeah," said another, "but Robby could have gotten separated from us almost anywhere."

"It's been an hour and a half since lunch," said Robby's dad, looking anxiously at his watch. "I think we should split up into two groups in order to cover more ground, and each group should have a leader that's familiar with this area; we don't want anyone else getting lost. If we do get out of sight of one another, let's rendezvous back at the mouth of the valley, where we ate lunch. I'll take Peter and four guys with me and the rest of you men go together."

The whole time while they were talking, Peter watched their back trail, in hopes he'd see Robby, but there was no sign of him. The men formed the search parties, and soon had turned around to go back the way they'd come.

Meanwhile, Robby had been going back and forth in every direction, but he still didn't have a clue to where everyone had gone. By now he'd made so many twists and turns that nothing looked even vaguely familiar anymore, and he wasn't sure he'd be able to find his way back to the main trail. Plus, it had begun to snow, and the visibility was starting to get pretty bad.

Suddenly, Robby's heart jumped into his throat, because to his horror he realized he had just driven his snow machine over a cliff! His engine's high-pitched scream of protest matched his own, as with its track spinning wildly in midair, it plummeted into a vast ravine. Losing hold of the handlebars on the way down, Robby was mercifully tossed clear of his heavier machine, which landed with a loud crash. His breath was knocked out of him, and he lay there gasping like a fish out of water.

While he panted for air, Robby's mind automatically checked for aches and pains. He discovered he was still in one piece, unlike his machine.

From where he lay he could see that it hadn't faired as well, and was pretty busted up. It was half buried in the snow, and laying on its side. The windshield was smashed in pieces, and one ski was bent like a pretzel. The engine had died, when it hit the ravine bottom, so he had no idea if it would still run. However, with the ruined ski he knew there was no way he'd be able to drive it out.

Chapter 4

Alone

The silence was intense. For the first time, he understood he was completely lost, and it was unlikely that anyone would ever be able to find him as long as he remained down in the hole. Also, without his dad or Peter to help him, he knew he'd have to get himself out of the ravine, and back to where the trucks were parked. He wasn't at all sure he could do that alone! He felt dazed from his fall, and found it hard to think about what he should do next.

Robby peered up toward the top of the ridges surrounding him, and groaned. *It's impossible! I'll never make it!* He thought, feeling hopeless, sad, and tired. The shock of his situation began to cause a few tears to trickle down his cheeks. Angrily, he brushed them away with the back of his snowmobile gloves, while thinking *I'm not going to cry! I'm not going to quit! I am going to get out!*

Slowly he crawled over to his snow-machine, and using it for support he was able to stand, but the snow was so soft he immediately sank down to above his knees. Again he felt overwhelmed by fear, but he knew that he couldn't stay where he was. He glanced once more uphill to check his direction, and began the difficult climb out.

As he trudged ahead, a verse from Psalms, which his mom had taught him, came to mind: "What time I am afraid, I will trust in Thee." He began to say it with each struggling step. "What time I am afraid I will trust in Thee." "What time I am afraid, I will trust in Thee!" Each time he repeated the verse, he felt calmer, and stronger, and more hopeful.

After a short distance though, he was out of breath, so he paused to look ahead, and see how much farther it was to the top. Discouragement draped itself like a cloak over his shoulders. The edge of the ridge still looked just as far away as it had when he had started! From there he lifted his gaze to the darkening sky, and he wondered again if he was going to get out of this jam. *What if they don't find me tonight? There's nothing for me to eat or drink, and no way to keep warm.*

Just thinking about food made his stomach growl, and he was pretty thirsty, too. However, he knew better than to eat snow to quench his thirst. Its freezing temperature would cool him to the core, and he could quickly become hypothermic.

Robby looked up toward the top of the ridge once more, and decided he'd better stay moving.

In spite of the energy it took to climb, he began to shiver. Both his hands and feet felt like ice. He'd read stories about people that had gotten lost, and ended up with frostbite. The frostbite had been so bad that noses, ears, fingers, toes, or occasionally, even whole hands or feet had to be cut off. He decided not to think about that, because at this point there wasn't much he could do anyway.

Robby slogged on for a while through the deep snow. Every few strides he would look ahead to make sure he was going in the right direction. However, after getting more and more depressed by his slow progress, Robby decided not to look toward the top of the ridge anymore. Instead, he just dragged one foot after the other, and repeated his verse for comfort.

After what seemed like a long time, Robby couldn't resist a peek at the ridge-top. He was relieved to see he had come quite a ways. However, even with the positive progress, he was still anxious. *It's getting dark fast and I'm only about halfway to the top of the hill! What am I going to do?* Once again he felt like giving up. It seemed so much easier to just lie down in the snow; but he knew if he did, it would be the beginning of the end, and any hope of ever being rescued. Doggedly he put one tired leg in front of the other, and continued to drag himself toward the crest of the hill.

In the meantime, Peter was really getting worried. The group he was with had been searching for half an hour, and they still didn't have any idea where his best friend might be. *I'm so afraid something terrible has happened to him! What if we never find him?* Peter thought, a cold hard lump began to form in the pit of his stomach. He knew Robby's dad must be really worried, too, and probably felt even worse than he did.

Just then, they caught sight of the other group of men that had split off to search. Robby's dad waved his arm to signal them to stop. All the men gathered around and killed their engines, so they could talk about what they'd seen, but no one had anything to report.

"Since it's begun to get dark, and because of the new fallen snow, I think it would be best if a couple of you headed back to the trucks to go for help. Remember the lodge we passed on the way up? They have a phone there I'm sure they'll let you use, since our cell phones are useless in this area. If they're not open, just keep going until you find a place where you can make a call. While you do that, the rest of us will stay together, and continue to search for another half hour. Then whether we've found Robby or not, we'll have to head back to the trucks."

Everyone looked miserable as they nodded agreement, and decided who would stay and who would go. Robby's dad, Peter, and the rest of the guys sat watching the two men chosen to ride out. They gazed silently until they could no longer see them in the distance, and then together everyone bowed their heads and prayed, asking the Lord to help them find Robby. Peter said a loud "Amen!" at the end of the prayer. Then he added a silent plea from his heart. *Please, please, please help us find Robby soon!*

In the quiet moments before they started their snow machines, a few of the men alternately called, and then listened. They did this for a few minutes, but there were no return calls or cries. After a brief discussion on where and how to search, everyone in the group began the hunt for Robby again.

While everyone was searching, Robby had finally made it to within a couple of yards of the top. He was so tired he didn't think he could go on. His head was hanging low from the weight of his helmet, which he still wore. He hoped it, along with his facemask, would help keep his face and ears from freezing. His limbs ached, and felt like they weighed a ton. His breath was coming in short, shallow gasps, and his head felt like it was spinning.

What was that? He thought he'd heard something! It sounded like a couple of snow-machines.

"Help! Help!" Robby yelled at the top of his lungs, but even though he yelled as loud as he could the sound of the machines faded away, and he knew they were gone. Robby was dreadfully disappointed. It really began to look like he was not only lost, but he was going to stay lost.

He was near exhaustion, but the brief promise of rescue gave him a new burst energy and determination to keep on going. After all, where there were a couple of snow-machines, there might be more.

Within a few more minutes, he reached the top. However, the only things Robby could see were a few scraggly windblown trees, and a whole lot of snow. The mountaintops had disappeared behind threatening cloudbanks, and the only sounds were raspy breathes of wind. He had never felt so alone in all his life.

Robby cried out, "Dad! Peter! Where are you?"

Fearfully, he looked around him, and thought *I might not be rescued! What will I do if nobody finds me before nightfall?*

"Oh, Jesus, help!" he moaned.

At once, a deep peace settled over him, and he remembered a time, a couple of years ago, when his dad had taught him about winter survival. One of the things he had said was, "If you ever get caught out in frigid winter weather, remember that snow can be your friend." He could hear his dad's voice teaching him how to build an ice or snow shelter, to help protect him from the wind, and trap his body heat to keep him warm.

He recalled his dad's advice, which renewed his strength, and sense of purpose. In the fading light, he struggled a few more feet over to a little weather-beaten tree. On the side, away from the wind, he found a small cave-like pocket that could easily be made into a place to stay until help arrived. He piled up snow around the opening, and packed it down as tight as he could to form some walls. When he was finished, he crawled into the small cave he had made, and pulled his knees up to his chest.

From where Robby sat, with his back to the tree, he could see the base of a mountain range that looked like it went on forever. He knew that it didn't, and that somewhere on the other side was his home, and his mother. He wished now he'd told her he loved her before he'd left this morning.

As he waited, he comforted himself with the thought that his dad and Peter would be the last to give up searching for him in this vast frozen wilderness. If they didn't find him tonight, they'd search for him again tomorrow, and as many tomorrows as it might take.

I still feel cold, but I'm warmer than I was, he thought, *and boy I'm hungry! But what I most want to do is just sleep, even though I know I shouldn't.*

Chapter 5

Rescued

Just before Robby slipped into slumber, he jerked his head up sharply, thinking. *I really mustn't go to sleep! I can't. If I do, I might miss my dad.*

His snow cave had actually begun to feel warm and cozy, so again his head drooped down until the chin guard of his helmet rested on his chest. His eyes flickered with the effort to stay awake.

What was that? Had he heard the distant throb of snow-machine engines? At first, he wondered if he was imagining it, and he was so comfy that he didn't want to move, but the sounds seemed to get louder and louder.

Excitedly, Robby scrambled out of his cave, and looked around. In the gathering gloom he saw headlights, from a bunch of snow-machines, shining through the falling snow, and coming in his general direction. With all his might, he began to wave his arms and holler for help. At first, he couldn't tell if they had seen him, but suddenly, one machine zipped out ahead of the others. He knew it had to be his dad!

The group had almost given up hope. They were headed back toward the trucks, when Robby's dad thought he saw something moving out of the corner of his eye. Sure enough, there was a small figure in the distance! He turned his machine to check to see if it might be Robby, and not just some animal seeking shelter from the storm.

It was Robby! His heart leaped for joy, as he ripped across the snow, jumped off his machine, and pulled his son into his arms, holding him tight, helmet and all.

Peter zoomed up, along with the other men, and soon everyone was slapping Robby on the back, telling him how glad they were to see him.

"What happened to you, son? Where's your machine?" Robby's dad asked at last.

Sighing with relief, Robby briefly told his story. The men peered down into the ravine, but in the dim light, and through the falling snow, they couldn't even see the bottom.

"Never mind about your machine, we'll figure that out later. Right now we'd better get back to the truck, and get you warmed up. We need to let everyone know we found you, and that you're okay."

Robby's dad reached over, and broke the treetop of the little spruce that had sheltered his son. He needed to have a marker in order to find his way back to retrieve the mangled snow-machine. Everybody restarted their engines, and hurriedly headed back toward the rendezvous point.

Peter was thinking. *Thank You, Jesus, for helping us find Robby. Thank You for keeping him safe, and hearing my prayer.*

Robby's thoughts were just a blur, as he clung to his dad's broad back with all his might.

The tired group of snow-machiners roared into the parking lot where some search and rescue men were gathered, along with the two guys that had gone to get help. When everyone saw Robby on the back of his dad's machine, they let out a cheer.

There was an ambulance waiting, with some volunteer paramedics. Robby's dad agreed with them that his son should go in the ambulance to the hospital. They would check him out, get him warmed up, and give him something hot to drink. Everyone encouraged his dad and Peter to go with him, and promised to bring the remainder of the gear, and tow the machines back as quickly as they could.

Robby didn't protest the special treatment, because he was more cold and tired than he had ever been in his life. For once he didn't even have the energy to share his adventure with his best friend.

After paramedics tested him for hypothermia, frostbite, and shock, they gave both boys a hot drink and snack. They put Robby on a cot in the back of the ambulance, where he curled up under a warm blanket, and immediately fell asleep. Peter was nearly as exhausted, so they wrapped him in a blanket, too. Leaning up against Robby's dad, Peter was asleep in no time.

The boys woke up a little over an hour later when the ambulance stopped, and Robby was wheeled, still very groggy, into the emergency room. The boy's moms were there with serious looks on their faces, which rapidly turned to relief when they saw their sons. The doctors looked Robby over thoroughly, and confirmed he was going to be fine with some more food and rest.

The two families discussed meeting in the morning to talk over what had happened, and how to get Robby's machine out of the ravine. Soon everyone went home, thankful that the day had not ended in tragedy like some snow-machine trips do, during the hazardous Alaska winters.

The next morning, over breakfast, Robby told what happened, and how he'd turned to the Lord for peace and strength. However, when he reached the part where he flew off the edge of the cliff, you could hear his mother's sharp intake of breath and her quiet "Thank you, Lord."

When he'd finished telling his story, his mom gave him a hard hug and a kiss on the cheek. He figured from the way she was acting that he might get his favorite meals and desserts for at least a week.

Peter piped up and added, "The Lord heard our prayers—remember how we we prayed for safety?"

"You're right!" said Robby and his dad in unison, while everyone smiled at each other around the table.

After a few moments, Robby's dad turned to him and said, "Son, I'm sorry I didn't notice earlier that you'd gotten separated from the rest of us. I hope this experience won't sour you on snow-machine trips in the future."

"You don't have to worry about that," answered Robby. "I just hope Peter and I can go again with you soon."

Robby's dad laughed, and got up to give his son a big hug. "Don't worry about that. All the men agreed that both of you were great riders, and next time we'll do a better job of keeping track of each other. I think we all learned some valuable lessons from this trip."

The boys faces lit up with happiness, and anticipation at his words, and they readily began to plan where they would like to go the next time.

A few days later, after the storm had passed, some of the men went up on the mountain and found Robby's snow-machine buried under a fairly deep, new layer of snow. They were able to get it to start, then quickly changed out the bent ski, and installed a replacement for the broken windshield. Robby's dad, after a couple of tries, was able to ride up and out of the ravine.

After his dad got home, Robby called Peter with the news.

"Guess what? They brought my machine home! Dad says it still runs fine, and with the repairs it's as good as new!"

"I'm really glad," said Peter, "but I wonder when we'll get to go on our next snow-machine trip?"

"I don't know," said Robby. "I just hope that the next time I don't get lost again."

No one would get lost, but together Peter and Robby would face unexpected danger in the vast, untamed wilderness known as Alaska.

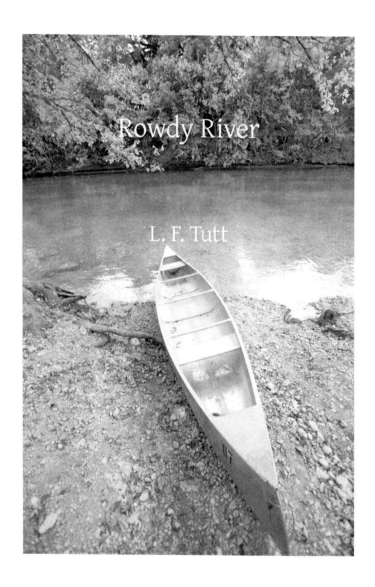

Rowdy River

L. F. Tutt

Chapter 1

Beaver, Bear, and Moose

Robby was hypnotized by the early morning sunlight, which sparkled and shimmered on the surface of Rowdy River. The fresh breeze that spun the surface of the gurgling water also swirled through his dark brown hair. It was a perfect Alaska spring day, with small, lime green leaves that flashed and fluttered against a bright blue sky. The air was warm, but still held a faint chill, which was a reminder that winter had melted away only a few weeks ago.

Multicolored gravel crunched under his feet as Robby walked over to sit on the front seat of the canoe that he, his dad, and his best friend Peter were going to use for their first ever float trip. They'd been waiting for weeks for the ice and snow to thaw, and conditions to be just right.

Just over an hour ago, they'd left home and driven until Robby's dad had turned off the main highway onto a narrow dirt road a mile and a quarter long. The "road," if you could call it that, was full of deep slippery ruts, and giant potholes. They had all been violently bounced and tossed around in the cab of the truck as Robby's dad navigated their way to the end of the road, and pulled onto a wide gravel beach.

The boys scrambled out of the truck, and began waving their arms around in an attempt to help guide Robby's dad as he reversed the pickup closer to the launch point. In *spite* of the boys' "help," he was able to back it into the right spot. They soon had the canoe off-loaded, and resting partly in the water. The boys loaded the gear, and put on their life jackets, and settled into the canoe. With a powerful push, Robby's dad broke the canoe free from shore, and steered them out into the swiftest part of the current.

"We're off!" hollered Peter in excitement.

Robby and his dad paddled fast to keep on course, while the riverbanks became a blur as they flew down the stream. Overhead, the sun played tag with them through the tall trees, which striped the water around them with shadow and light. There didn't seem to be any boulders or snags in this part of the creek, so all they had to do was keep the canoe moving with the flow of the water. The speed at which they were moving caused Peter to hang on white-knuckle tight, as they rocketed downstream.

Before long the river current slowed, the tree-lined hills flattened out, and large meadows became visible on both sides of the creek. Across the grassland, and over distant treetops, they could see the high snowcapped mountains, where just a few months ago Robby had been lost while snow-machining.

Abruptly, Peter pointed to his right and said, "Look, there's a beaver lodge, the biggest one I've ever seen!" Robby and his dad turned to look in the direction Peter gestured, and saw the massive mound nestled in a small pond.

"Hey, let's get out and investigate," suggested Peter.

"Yes, please dad, let's stop here," begged Robby.

Grinning, Robby's dad nosed the canoe into a side stream, and the boys piled out onto the shore. "Shh! don't make so much noise," Robby's dad whispered. "Let's try not to scare away the beaver."

The boys followed his example by creeping low and slow toward the lodge. In a few minutes they were close enough to see over the tops of some brush, and into the dark green waters of the pond.

Near where they were crouching was a large adult beaver with long, reddish brown fur, and a pancake-shaped tail. He swam industriously toward his home with a branch in his mouth. As they watched, he dragged the branch partway up onto the roof of his lodge.

"Look! He's eating some small twigs off the branch," whispered Robby.

Peter just nodded his head, fascinated by the sight of this funny creature. The beaver held the branch in paws that looked almost human in the way they gripped, turned, and held the tree limb.

All at once Peter felt a tickle in his nose! He rubbed it a couple of times, then pressed his finger up against the base, but it was too late. A huge sneeze ripped out! The startled beaver stopped eating, peered nearsightedly in their direction, and then smoothly slid down from the roof of his lodge into the water. To show them he was upset he gave a loud slap with his tail.

"Oops!" said Peter sheepishly.

"Way to go, meathead!" laughed Robby.

"That's okay," said Robby's dad, "it's time we got back on the river anyway."

When they were almost back to the canoe, Robby's dad stopped, and signaled for the boys to stand still and be quiet. Both of them froze in mid-stride, and in slow motion looked around to see what had caught his attention. Robby felt prickles of fear run down his spine! Not more than a hundred and fifty yards away, across the stream, was a golden colored grizzly bear. He was wandering across the meadowlands, sniffing the breeze as he lumbered in their direction. If the bear decided to cross the stream, he would come right by the canoe and straight up the path where they were standing.

Robby's dad decided not to try to scare it away with hand gestures and loud noises, in case that might cause it to charge. Instead he opted to stand very still. He hoped the grizzly would turn around and head back the way he had come, rather than cross the cold stream. Behind him he could hear the boys breathing in and out in short fearful puffs, as they waited to see what the bear would do next.

The moments seemed to drag as the grizzly continued to amble toward them. Robby's dad was just about to have the boys back away toward the tree line, when he heard the whine of a small outboard motor, and some loud male voices. The bear heard the same thing, and stopped to listen. He lifted his great snout to capture any scent on the breeze, and peered with his poor eyesight upriver. Suddenly, the big bear whirled around, and galloped back the way he'd come. He disappeared into the trees just as a boatload of fishermen motored by.

"Whew! That was close!" gasped Robby, looking at his friend with a bug-eyed stare.

"Wow!" Peter exclaimed.

"Well, boys, was that enough excitement for you?"

"More than enough, dad," Robby declared.

"Well, let's get in the canoe before that old bear decides to come back, okay?" The boys didn't need to be asked twice.

Once they were back on the creek, they could see that last autumn's heavy rains had forced it to change its course. Also, a lot of trees, bushes, and chunks of the riverbank had been washed down, and left behind during the flood.

"Do you see the damage the flood did?" asked Robby's dad. "We'll need to be really careful, and alert from now on," he cautioned. "We don't want to accidentally capsize the canoe on some underwater debris."

"I know I don't want to wind up in the creek," said Peter. "The water is super cold this time of year!"

"Yeah, there was still some ice here just a couple weeks ago, when we checked to see if the creek was ready to float," remembered Robby.

Just then, a flock of sandpipers lifted off a nearby sandbar, and flew higher and higher into the sky. They turned first one way, and then another in perfect formation until they disappeared from sight. Peter marveled in his heart at the wonder of God's creation, and the privilege he had to live in Alaska, where there was so much wild beauty to be seen.

Robby and his dad continued to paddle peacefully along, while the canoe floated gracefully in time with the current.

As they rounded a wide bend in the river, they unexpectedly found themselves face-to-face with a huge, coffee-colored, mother moose! She was standing right in the middle of the water about two hundred feet ahead, watching her twin calves swim across the current toward the far shore.

Robby's dad thought. *Uh-oh, a mother moose! We better watch out! Maybe if we give her enough space she'll get out of our way.* This moose, however, was very startled by their sudden appearance. She chose not to flee; instead she raised her hackles, flattened her ears, and moved her body between her babies and the canoe. Still, this would have been okay if she had just stood there, but instead she charged upstream right at them.

"Back paddle, quick!" shouted Robby's dad, as he and Robby strained to keep the canoe away from the moose.

"Now, paddle hard!" his dad hollered. The bow of the canoe swung toward shore and possible safety, if they could make it in time. Nobody looked back when they jumped out of the canoe, and ran to hide in a grove of large trees. They were very thankful when they realized the moose hadn't followed them, but instead turned, and herded her little calves toward the opposite shore.

As soon as the moose were out of sight, Robby's dad ran over to see what had become of the canoe, since no one had taken time to tie it off. Happily, an eddy in the stream had held it against the shore, so it hadn't drifted away. He went down and secured it to a nearby log, and called to the boys saying, "Come on, the coast is clear."

Robby and Peter walked down to the beach, hearts still pounding from their second encounter with a large animal in a short space of time. They plunked down on a hunk of driftwood where the canoe was now tied, and attempted to catch their breath, and wait for their knees to stop shaking.

"Whew," said Robby's dad, "that was a close one!"

"Yeah," Robby reflected. "I've never seen a moose do that before. They are so enormous up close, and it's pretty scary when they get mad."

His dad said, "Do you remember last winter when the neighbor's dog was stomped by an angry moose? People always think it's just the bears they have to watch out for in Alaska, but moose can be really ornery if surprised or cornered—or if they are protecting their young." The boys nodded solemnly in response.

Back in the boat and out on the creek, Peter listened to the dips and swooshes of the paddles, which made the canoe dart like an arrow through the water. He looked at his friend seated in front of him and thought about what a great guy he was. *It's so much fun doing things with Robby; he really is my best friend. Plus, he and his dad have been there for me ever since my dad passed away two years ago.*

Peter became lost in his thoughts, and didn't detect the radical changes, which had taken place in the river, until he noticed how much harder Robby and his dad had to work to keep the canoe on course. The current of the creek had gotten much stronger, and it had become more and more difficult to control the canoe. Now they faced the danger of being smashed into some huge boulders in the middle of the violent water.

Along the shore the terrain had also changed, from low dirt banks to granite cliffs which towered and, loomed high overhead. The canoe suddenly plunged from bright daylight into their shadowy gloom. In addition, Peter was aware of a sharp change in the downward slant of the creek, which made roaring rapids out of small ripples.

Robby's dad began to shout directions over the increased rumble of the creek, "Quick son, paddle hard on your right! Paddle faster! Now paddle hard on your left! On the left! Harder! Harder! Peter! Robby—hang on!"

The canoe pitched wildly, like a bucking bronco, and some water splashed over its bow. Then it tipped hard toward the right, and Peter's face was only inches away from a gigantic, craggy rock. Robby and his dad managed to keep the boat upright, but just barely.

It seemed like they were going to thrash and twist around in the wild water forever. However, almost as rapidly as the river had become rowdy, it calmed once again into a sleepier rhythm. Soon they floated out of the shadows to play hide-and-seek again with the tree-filtered sunlight.

"Wow! That was intense," said Robby's dad, breathing hard. "I've been looking forward to shooting those rapids, but I couldn't have done it without your great effort, son!"

A big grin split Robby's face at his father's praise.

Chapter 2

The Winding Trail

"Say guys, I think it would be an excellent time for us to go ashore at the next good spot we find, so we can all relax in the sun. While we're there, we can eat the delicious looking lunches your mothers packed for us."

"Great idea," eagerly exclaimed Peter, always ready to eat.

"Goes double for me!" replied Robby with a grin.

They continued down the creek, first one boy and then the other pointing out likely places to stop, but there was always something wrong with each site. One didn't have any large rocks or driftwood where they could sit and rest; another was almost totally in the shade. They found another likely spot and drew close in order to land, but something smelled really rotten, so they decided not to go ashore there, either.

Finally, they spied a wide sandbar bathed in sunlight, with a large, gray driftwood log that was perfect to sit on. As a tempting bonus, they saw a narrow, well-used animal trail meandering off into the woods.

Robby cried eagerly, "Hey, let's stop here."

"Yeah, and right after we eat our lunch, I want to go exploring up that trail to see where it leads," said Peter.

Robby's dad steered the canoe toward shore, glad that they'd finally found a place to take a break. The boys got out and began leaping and jumping around, very happy to be able to stretch their legs.

"Hey dad, what's for lunch?" asked Robby, as everyone took off their life jackets.

"Well, let's see," his dad said, going over to lift the waterproof rucksack from the bottom of the canoe. "Hmm, it looks like we have some sandwiches to eat—two roast beef and cheese apiece—three slightly squished bananas, and a large bag of homemade chocolate chip cookies." Robby's dad rummaged around some more and found three cans of root beer soda, which he handed to Peter saying, "Here's the pop, would you go put it in the creek to chill? Make sure to put it where it won't float away. While he's doing that, Robby, you and I can get the rest of the meal unpacked and set out."

Soon they were all seated on the old log. Peter noticed that Robby and his dad had bowed their heads in silent prayer, so he did the same, truly thanking the Lord from the bottom of his heart for the great time he was having, and for the food, of course. After prayer they all eagerly chomped down their lunches.

Robby's dad finished his lunch first and asked, "Didn't you guys say you wanted to see where that trail might lead?"

"Yes," they said in unison, putting the remains of their lunch back into the rucksack.

"Well boys, let's go then!" Peter and Robby didn't need a second invitation. They immediately leaped up, from the log, and took off running.

"Race you!" yelled Peter over his shoulder as he dashed away.

"Hey, wait up," called Robby, quickly sprinting up the twisting path after his friend.

Robby's dad was still putting things away. He shouted to them as they zipped up the trail, "Stay in sight so we don't get separated!"

"Okay!" they shouted, without a backward glance.

The trail led them to the top of a fairly steep hill, where they stopped to look back over the way they had come. They discovered they could see down across an open portion of meadow, and all the way to the sandbar where they'd eaten their lunch. Below them, Robby's dad was walking slowly up the trail surveying the surrounding area. It looked like he wasn't going to catch up to them for a minute or two, so the boys plopped down to wait.

While they relaxed, Robby asked, "I wonder what made this trail?"

"Oh, I don't know," joked Peter, "probably rabid squirrels, wily wolves, and mad moose!" Robby just rolled his eyes in pretend disgust, and gave his friend a small shove.

"Hey, what's the big idea?" asked Peter, as he mischievously tackled his friend. His return shove was hard enough to knock Robby flat on his back. Cheerfully they wrestled around, and were soon covered in dirt, with leaves and twigs stuck in their hair.

Just then, Robby's dad reached them. He said with a chuckle, "Come on you two, we haven't got all day." He continued to hike, so the boys hurriedly got up, dusted off, and trooped after him. When they'd caught up, he said, "Why don't we walk quietly for awhile? Maybe we'll be able to spot some more wild animals if we do."

After a short time, he paused and pointed down at some animal tracks, which came out of a small clearing to the right. "Do you know what kind of mammal belongs to these prints?" The boys examined the soft dirt near their feet, and found impressions of four small toes above a larger pad in the center. The tracks went up the path in the same direction they were going.

"I think they were left by a fox or maybe a wolf," answered Peter.

"Yes, they're fox; you can tell by their size, and how short the distance is between the animal's steps. Now, who can tell me when they were made?"

"Maybe sometime earlier today?" queried Robby after examining them for a few more moments.

"Yes, you're right. Most likely it would have been early in the morning. Generally, wood and field animals are on the move at that time, and they tend to rest during the hot, bright part of the day."

"Dad, do you think we might be able to track the fox, see where it was going, and maybe even find its lair?"

"Possibly," his father said.

"I suppose this means I'll have to be quiet some more," Peter declared with a grin.

Robby and his dad just smiled back at him. Everyone took care not to step on the fox tracks, as they followed the twisting trail through dense forest. They were now far enough from the creek that they couldn't hear its merry song, and this deep in the woods even the breezes were still. They were all very thankful it was too early in the year for mosquitoes to have hatched.

Along the path they came upon the tracks of other creatures, which had crossed or passed that way— squirrels, rabbits, mice, and even the strange trail made by a porcupine dragging his prickly tail. However, through all of these threaded the tracks of the fox.

All at once, they came into a more open sunlit area split by a small babbling brook. The sun was dappling the surface of a pool, formed where the trail and brook met. They could see a jumble of animal tracks down by the water, including some fairly fresh yearling moose tracks. This was obviously a favorite watering hole for the woodland creatures in the area. They jumped the tiny stream just above the pool, and they expected to pick up the fox tracks on the other side. However even though they went a ways up the path, and searched carefully all around, they couldn't find them anywhere.

"I don't think the fox crossed to this side," said Robby's dad after a thorough search. "Let's go back, and see if we can find where he turned off."

"I hope we didn't lose her after all this time," said Peter, as he wiped his brow with his sleeve.

"Me too!" chimed in Robby.

They leaped back to the other bank, and began carefully looking upstream and down for the fox tracks. There were so many footprints left by other animals, who'd come to drink and refresh themselves, that it was hard to tell which was which. Finally, Robby called out excitedly, "I found them!"

His dad and Peter, who'd been searching downstream, jogged up to where Robby was standing. There under a large fern, which drooped over the trail, was a very clear fox print.

Robby's dad said in a whisper, "I think from here on we'd better be really quiet. If we are lucky enough to find the fox in its den, we don't want to scare it or make it nervous. Keep your eyes open, and no talking, and we just might find that fox yet." Robby and Peter promised to do what he said, making exaggerated zipping motions across their lips to seal the deal.

The trail took them along the edge of the brook, deeper into the woods. After about a half mile, they noticed a faint pathway leading up another hillside into the woods. The tracks of the fox turned aside there. Robby's dad held up his hand to motion them to stop, while he cautiously moved around. He peered through the undergrowth and trees, trying to see if he could spot a den.

Finally, after what seemed like a long time to the eager boys, Robby's dad smiled, and motioned for them to stand near him. He crouched down a little until he was about the same height as they were, and pointed. Speaking very softly he said, "Look straight up the hill, using the edge of this birch tree as a guide. Just about three-fourths of the way up, you'll see a dark hole under a rocky overhang, with some dirt pushed out in front. That is the fox's lair." The boys took turns looking, and they were finally able to see the den, but the fox wasn't in sight.

"Dad, do you think the fox is in there?" whispered Robby.

"I think so, and since we've come all this way, why don't we just rest here for a while, and see if she comes out?" The boys nodded and stood silently waiting.

When they were just about to give up, their patience was rewarded. All of a sudden, a bright orange face tipped with a small black nose popped out of the mouth of the den, and sniffed the air. They were downwind of the fox, but they knew it had keen eyesight, so they were very careful not to move. The fox didn't appear to be wary; instead she seemed quite content to continue sniffing the air, and catching a few rays of sunlight, that was filtered by the upper canopy of the trees. When the fox turned and disappeared from sight into the den, Robby's dad motioned to the boys that it was time to go.

Peter and Robby pulled long faces, but after a last look, they followed Robby's dad down the trail. They walked in silence until they were back to the main path. Then they all stopped and talked excitedly.

"Wow, that was so cool!" exclaimed Robby. "Yeah, it was fun getting to see a fox in its den!" agreed

Peter. "Didn't we do a great job of tracking today?" he added.

"Yes, I'm very proud of you guys, but speaking of tracks, let's see who can make the fastest ones back to the canoe." With that, Robby's dad took off running at top speed. He zigzagged and leaped down the trail with the boys in quick pursuit. In no time they had crashed their way back to the sandbar, with Robby's dad the winner by a hair.

After they caught their breath, they began to gather everything together to stow back in the canoe. It was then Peter remembered their pop still chilling in the creek.

"Here Robby, catch!" he said, as he threw one can to his friend. He then walked over to hand another one to Robby's dad, before opening the top on his own.

"Boy this pop sure tastes good after our hike," said Peter, letting out little burps as he spoke. Robby's dad just smiled, shook his head and said, "Okay boys, let's go."

They took another look around to make sure they had all their garbage in the pack, and that the sandbar was as clean as when they'd landed. After their final check, they put their life jackets on, and climbed back into the canoe. This time Peter got to sit in the bow; it was now his turn to paddle.

Chapter 3

Overboard

Soon they'd left their picnic spot behind. As they floated downstream, they all enjoyed the beautiful scenery, and the many changes in Rowdy River. Over the next two hours, they went through more rapids, drifted past meadows, and were carried through quiet woodland areas. They observed a pair of eagles, which soared high above a towering cliff, and watched an incredible dipper bird. The dipper walked underwater to catch insects for its lunch. They saw more evidence of beaver, and watched a porcupine climbing a tree to strip it of its bark.

After they had rounded a couple more bends in the river, they were surprised to meet up with the guys they'd seen go by earlier in the motorboat; the men stood on the riverbank fly fishing.

"Hello there, what are you fishing for?" Robby's dad called out.

"Grayling and rainbow trout!" shouted one of the men.

"Have you caught anything yet?"

"No! Not yet."

"Well, good luck!"

The men just smiled, and kept on casting their flies.

Robby's dad said. "Even though we've had an early spring, I doubt grayling or rainbows would be this far upriver. Maybe we can come back in a few weeks, and find out for ourselves where the fish might be."

"That would be great," the boys said enthusiastically.

Peter began to daydream about what it would be like to catch his first fish of the year. While he paddled, he pictured himself fighting a big grayling that dragged his line out yard after yard. In his mind he could see its silver sides flash in the sunlight as it tried to get away, but Peter was sure, with *his* skill, the grayling would be no match for him. He envisioned himself proudly delivering a huge three pound grayling to his mom for her to cook over a campfire. Then a little later, after he'd eaten his fish with her yummy homemade potato salad, and a big bag of chips, he'd toast some marshmallows for dessert and …

He had been so busy with his thoughts that he hadn't noticed the underwater debris just ahead, before it was too late.

A loud bang echoed across the creek! The canoe had slammed into a large, partially sunken snag. It hit so hard that the bow pitched wildly up into the air. Robby was thrown onto his hands and knees into the bottom of the canoe, but Peter was tossed out headfirst into the rushing stream!

At once the frigid water closed over his head. The current tumbled him around until he wasn't even sure which way was up. There hadn't been enough time for him to get a decent breath of air. He opened his eyes, but all he could see was foaming, green water.

In his fear he thrashed around with his hands and feet trying to find the bottom of the creek in order to stand up. Surely it wasn't that deep in this area, but try as he might he could find nothing to grab hold of or anywhere to stand. *Lord, help!* He cried in his heart.

The cold water was mind numbing, and the pressure in his lungs was becoming so intense that he didn't think he'd be able to hold his breath for much longer. Then he remembered what Robby's dad had taught him—*don't fight the water! Just relax, and you should naturally pop up to the surface, especially when you're in a life jacket.* Peter willed himself to relax, and immediately felt his body rising. All of a sudden, his head broke the surface of the creek, and he was able to take a huge, much-needed breath of wonderful air.

However, when he looked around, he realized he was being swept around a bend of the river, and rapidly carried downstream. Robby, his dad, and the canoe were nowhere in sight! *Where are they?* He wondered. *Did the canoe capsize? Were we all thrown out?*

Fear gripped him, especially since it was hard to move about in his life jacket. He needed to get to shore, but the fast current was extremely strong, and though he made a lot of effort, it continued to carry him down the middle of the stream.

He realized he was terribly cold. His teeth began to chatter, and it felt like his hands and feet were beginning to get numb. Just ahead, he saw a large boulder, which thrust up out of the water. Around its sides the water churned and frothed, and he was headed straight toward it, fast!

Peter tried with all his might to swim toward shore away from the huge rock, but he could see that the river was relentless in its attempt to pull him in that direction. Then suddenly, he slammed into it. His whole body received a violent jolt, and he was spun around. However, he seemed to be okay, even though he was shook up. His life preserver had protected him from the boulder's sharp edges, but he knew he might not be so lucky next time.

Peter tried to relax enough to think. His first thought became a prayer of desperation. *Lord, what should I do?* Miraculously, as he looked ahead, he spied a solution that might help get him out of the water. In the stream, a little to his right, was a partially submerged log wedged against other pieces of driftwood, and pointing straight out into the river. If only he could swim over just a little bit more, he might have a chance to grab hold of it, and stop his unwanted progress downstream.

With the last of his strength, he thrashed his arms, and kicked with his legs toward the log. In response to his efforts, the current released its hold. He found himself being carried toward the debris, and seconds later he had the log in his grasp. It was very slippery with brown slime, and he found it hard to hang on to. However, when he relaxed, the water just naturally held him in place. It was just like what had happened with the canoe earlier in the day, when they had fled from the moose.

Peter's breathing was shallow as he rested his head against the old tree, and now the cold really overwhelmed him. He wished he could just get to shore, but he was afraid to move, afraid he'd be swept away again.

Chapter 4

Saved

He hadn't been against the snag long when he heard a shout, "Peter, we're coming!"

"Help!" he hollered back with all his might, but neither Robby nor his dad could hear him over the sound of the river.

Robby's dad had barely managed to keep the canoe upright, and quite a bit of water had come in, and was slopping around. With Robby still down in the bottom of the canoe, he had paddled it as speedily as possible downriver. It had seemed like an eternity, and both Robby and his dad had sent up frantic SOS's to God. They were so relieved, when they spotted Peter clinging to a log by the shore.

When Robby's dad first saw him, he was afraid that he might be unconscious or had even drowned, and had just washed up against the log like a piece if driftwood. However, as he drew closer, he could see that Peter had a tight grip on the log, and seemed to be alert. His heart leaped with joy! "Praise You, Lord!" he cried.

When they drew alongside of Peter, Robby's dad instructed him to let go of the log. Robby grabbed him by his life jacket, and as carefully as he could, Robby's dad paddled the short distance to shore.

"Are you okay?" Robby asked, as he helped pull Peter up onto the beach.

"Yeah," Peter said weakly, "but I am really c–c-cold."

"Just relax a moment while we dump the water out of the canoe," said Robby's dad. Then we'll be on our way to the campground. I'm sure that in no time we'll get you there, dried out, and warmed up."

Peter barely had time to register what he had said, before they were back in the canoe, and traveling fast.

"I'm so glad I made you boys wear life jackets!"

"Me too!" was Peter's muffled reply; his face smashed up against the duffle bag, as he rested in the bottom of the canoe.

"Let's see how quick this old boat will go!" Robby's dad said, in a hurry to get Peter down river to the landing. He knew that Peter wasn't out of danger. He'd been in the cold water long enough to be chilled to the bone.

Robby and his dad paddled as hard and fast as they could, which made the canoe lunge forward several feet with each trust. With the brisk current of the river they made good time.

Peter heard the surge and splash of the water around the boat as they shot downstream. However, he was so cold that he could hardly think, and he shivered uncontrollably. Robby and his dad didn't let up their rapid pace, until they drove the canoe up onto the campground beach. Peter heard a loud sound like fingernails on a chalkboard, as the bottom of the canoe skidded over the rocks and sand, and came to an almost immediate stop. Robby and his dad jumped out onto the shore, and pulled the canoe the rest of the way up to secure it.

"Robby, go see if you can find your mom, while I get Peter out of the canoe and headed toward the truck."

Robby ran up a path that turned and twisted for a short distance through the woods, until it emptied into a large parking lot. The lot was full of RVs, camp trailers, cars, and trucks. He spotted his mom and Peter's mom, who was also there, and rushed over to them.

"Please come quickly. We had an accident and Peter almost drowned. He needs to get out of his wet clothes and into the truck to get warm!"

Peter's mom cried out, "Is he okay?"

"Yes, but he needs help, now!"

"You go to your son; I'll get out some dry clothes and start the truck warming up," said Robby's mom.

Peter's mom didn't hesitate, but swiftly followed Robby back down the trail. When she met up with Peter and Robby's dad, she put her arms around her son, and gave him a big hug. Then she turned, and led him the final distance to the truck.

Once Peter was in dry clothes and partially thawed out, his mother left him to talk with the other adults.

"How did it happen?" she asked.

"It's a long story," Robby's dad replied. "I think it would be best if we talked about it later, when the boys can be in on the conversation."

After a little more discussion, Peter's mom went back to the truck.

"I-I didn't know you were going to be here to m-m-meet us!" said Peter through his still chattering teeth.

"I worked it out with Robby's parents last night after you'd gone to bed," said his mom, rubbing Peter's arms and back to get his circulation going. "I decided not to tell you, so it would be a surprise. I drove Robby's mom over to get their truck, where you guys left it upstream, and then we drove down to be here when you arrived."

"I wondered how we were going to get the truck."

After about another half hour, the very hot air from the truck heater did its magic, and Peter no longer shivered and shook.

"When do we get to eat?" Peter asked his mom.

"I guess you are going to be okay if you're hungry," said his mother, as she laughed with relief. They stayed a few more minutes, and then his mom said, "Do you want to go see if maybe someone got a campfire going? We brought along a picnic of hot dogs, potato salad, chips, marshmallows, and pop."

"Yum," Peter said, as he smacked his lips in anticipation. They followed the trail back to the river, where Robby and his dad had started a campfire. The sight of its orange glow was cheery and bright.

"Hey!" said Robby's mom to Peter. "Are you already warm enough to be out here?"

"Yeah, the heater in the truck thawed me out pretty fast."

"Well, then, I think the only thing we need now is for you and Robby to go cut some sticks for roasting the 'dogs' and marshmallows." The boys didn't need to be told twice. They eagerly trotted along the creek to a big stand of willow and alder bushes.

While the boys were busy, their parents set out the picnic food on a rustic camp table, and then sat on logs by the fire to wait for the boys to return with the sticks.

When Peter and Robby reached the bushes, they took out their pocket knives—Peter had to dry his on his pants—and carefully looked over branches for size, length, and strength. They wanted to cut the best roasting sticks ever. Peter found just the branch he was looking for and said, "Look at this one, it's got a two-pronged fork on one end. That way I'll be able to roast at least two hot dogs or marshmallows at once."

Robby laughed as he held up the one he'd just finished; it had a fork in it, too.

"Hey, how many of these do we need to make?"

"Let's see, I think we need five altogether," answered Robby, as he busily carved a couple more sticks for his mom and dad. Soon the boys had all they needed, and turned to follow the path back to camp.

Chapter 5

Campfire Time

When they returned to the picnic area, they were welcomed by the rich smoky smell of the fire. They sat on a log Robby's dad had drawn close to the flames, and watched the sparks float upward into the evening sky. The heat from the campfire reached out to them, with an invitation of warmth, and kept the few mosquitoes away that had arrived as the sun dropped lower in the sky.

All of a sudden, Robby began to wave his arms around and make sounds like he was going to choke.

"What *are* you doing?" laughed Peter.

"The smoke's in my eyes, and it's made me cough," replied Robby, as he moved to the other side of the fire. However, he hadn't been in his new spot for more than a minute, before he had to jump up and move again.

"You must be beautiful," teased his friend, "because they say that smoke follows beauty."

"Yeah, right!" said Robby between coughs, moving back to where he'd started.

"Boys, I think the coals are ready. Let's go get our hot dogs."

The boys grabbed their sticks and ran to the table. They filled their plates with the other food, and got their buns ready before going back to roast their hot dogs. They carefully placed them over the embers and hot coals of the fire, knowing from experience that they would cook and not burn as easily there. They turned them this way and that, until every side was slightly browned, and the juices were dripping out. Quickly they removed them from the fire, and stuck them into the buns, and began to chow down like they hadn't eaten in days, instead of just a few hours.

"Hey boys, did you forget something?" The boys stopped chewing, and Peter said around his mouthful of hot dog, "We forgot to pray!"

"That's right," Robby's dad said, "and I think we should, because we really have a lot to be thankful for tonight."

"Dear Lord," Robby's dad prayed, "we thank You for this day, for the beauty of Your creation, and for this food. Most of all, we thank You for keeping us safe on the river. We thank You especially for rescuing Peter, and keeping the boat from capsizing. You are so good to us. We praise You, Jesus. Amen!"

"Amen," echoed the boys and their moms.

After the boys had consumed a couple hot dogs apiece, and at least two helpings of everything else, Peter said, "I'm ready to cook a few marshmallows."

"Yeah, me too!" said Robby, as he ripped the bag open, and grabbed a fist full of the white puffy things. They put them on their forked roasting sticks, and held them cautiously down near the red-hot coals.

"Ack!" exclaimed Peter, when his marshmallows burst into flames. He blew on them, but it was too late; they were black, with big crispy bubbles all over them.

"Yuck!" was all he could say as he pulled them off and threw them into the fire. Peter put on a couple more and sat watching them more attentively, hoping his would become the same soft, caramel color as Robby's.

"I think mine are done!" Robby said proudly, making a big deal out of eating them in front of Peter. "Mmm, these are *so* good," he said, as he sucked every last creamy bit off his fingers. "Too bad yours burned," he continued, flashing a marshmallow smeared grin at his friend.

"You won't be able to brag for long," replied Peter, as he slowly twirled his marshmallows a few more times until they were a perfect golden brown.

Robby's dad groaned with pleasure, and patted his distended stomach saying, "I don't know how you boys can keep eating. I'm so full I can't squeeze even a marshmallow in with the rest of what I've eaten."

Peter said, "I bet Robby and I can still eat at least a dozen more." Robby nodded his head in agreement, his mouth, once again, too full to talk.

Everyone rested on the logs as they watched the remains of the daylight turn to a peachy glow. Now, the warmth of the fire felt extra good, as the chill of an Alaska spring night crept up from the gurgling creek.

"Well," Peter's mom said, "now that you boys are full and your mouths are empty enough to talk, how about telling us about what happened out on the river today? While you were cutting the hot dog sticks, Robby's dad filled us in on all the neat critter adventures you had. But we still don't know what happened that caused the accident."

Until that moment Peter hadn't really thought over what *had* happened; but now that he did, he felt embarrassed and sheepish.

"The accident was really my fault," he said. "I wasn't paying attention like you had told me to, sir," Peter said, looking at Robby's dad. "I was daydreaming about fishing, and eating, and … well I just didn't pay attention. By the time I did, it was too late to warn you about the driftwood snag. Since it was my fault, I'm just glad I was the only one that got thrown into the river."

"Well, that's what I kind of figured had happened. It was a tough lesson that thankfully ended well, but next time we'll all be more careful, won't we?"

"You bet," the boys said in unison.

The night was cool enough now, that even with the fire everyone was starting to get chilled—roasted on the front, but their backs cold as ice. So, they began to pack up what was left of the picnic and to carry it to the trucks. Once everything but the canoe and paddles were stowed, Robby's dad moved his truck over to the landing. Together with the boys, he got the boat loaded and tied down.

"Dad, could we go down to the creek one last time?" asked Robby.

"Yeah, but only for five minutes; remember, we have an hour's drive home, and then we still have the canoe and all this stuff to put away."

"Okay," the boys said, as they turned and ran back down to the creek to stand side by side listening to its quiet babble. Then they found a few flat stones, which they began to skim across the peaceful water. Through the tall spruce and cottonwood trees that lined the opposite shore, they could see a half moon had begun to rise and cast its hazy glow.

Robby remarked in a soft voice that was almost a whisper, "I'm sure glad you didn't get badly hurt or drown today!"

"Yeah," said Peter quietly. "I know that for a while I wasn't too sure what was going to happen. I prayed pretty hard, though, and the Lord must have heard me 'cause here I am."

"I guess next time we *will* be more careful," said Robby as he turned away from the creek, putting his arm around his friend's shoulder as they walked back along the path.

The Greatest Adventure of All

If you are looking for the greatest adventure of all,
make Jesus your friend and Savior.

We are told in the Bible that God loves us and that
He sent His son Jesus to set us free from all the bad
things that have been done to us or that we have
done. If we ask, Jesus comes into our life, and then
we begin a wonderful journey with Him.

To get to know Jesus just pray this simple prayer:

Dear Jesus,

*Please come into my life and set me free
from sin and heal my heart.*

I want this life adventure with you.

In Jesus name, Amen!

CPSIA information can be obtained at www.ICGtesting.com
Printed in the USA
LVOW040018091211

258499LV00001B/1/P